From the bestselling sapphic author of Lady Venom Takes a Mistress, comes a nautical tale of romance between a fierce siren and a runaway sailor girl.

The ships hold the men, and the men are the sirens' meals.

Luring sailors with their songs and feasting upon the men's bodies is a siren's sacred calling within the sugar seas. But what happens when a woman is aboard? A siren has never seen a girl before and her beauty calls to her. Will their love survive the terrors of the waves?

Or is their story another tragedy at the claws of the sirens of the sugar seas?

Sirens of the Sugar Seas

A SAPPHIC MARITIME STORY

KAT BLACKTHORNE

Preface

This is a 17,000 word sapphic monster novella and is intended for mature audiences of 18 and up. Please see content details at the beginning of book and on author site.

Swim cautiously into the waters of the sugar seas... content warnings include: death, human + siren love, body gore, ocean horror, use of tentacles, sharks, fire, breakup trauma, and men.

Enjoy with rum, as a bedtime story, a quick beach read, or lunch break treat.

THE GIRL

I had to get away from her. For her I would bury myself in the sand, I'd throw myself off the tallest building, I'd tie a rock to my ankle and sink to the bottom of the cursed ocean.

"Why do you keep touching it? My hair is nothing special, just plain old brown. Like dirt or something filthy." The girl I loved giggled.

Pain and indignation shot through my heart as her silky strands wove through my fingers. "Rummy, don't you see that it's the same shade as the boat dock after the fiercest of storms? The dock always survives and graces us with the most gorgeous shade of umber. That's what color your hair is."

Escape. I had to escape her.

Gulls squawked overhead and the salty smell of the ocean sat heavy on my reddening skin. Coward. I was a fucking coward. A crazy fucking coward, I realized, as I stared down at the ship, willing my legs to move.

"I'm here to respond to the ad for a seaman," I said to myself, willing my voice into a gruff, unnatural tone. Sailors stayed at the inn I worked at, and I'd memorized their tone, the way they'd walked, and often imitated them to make Rummy laugh. But now it wasn't for show, or to impress the girl who didn't love me back. No, this was my grand audition. My role? Spineless lady sailor.

Which would work against me more, I wondered? The fact that I'd never set foot on a boat in my life, or the tiny detail that I was a woman, and women never sailed. I was betting it was the latter.

But I'd pulled my hair back into a tight knot at the nape of my neck, stolen a hat, britches, boots, and a men's shirt from the lost items at my small seaside inn. If they didn't look too closely, they might not notice. I looked like a scrawny sailor boy if you didn't look too hard and if I caved my spine inward to hide my breasts. Shoving my hands in my pockets, I sucked in a breath and creaked across the sandy and splintery dock.

Men bustled aboard the modestly sized sailboat. Or was it a ship? What was the difference? Hell if I knew. Maybe it should have crossed my mind that not knowing the answer to the most basic of sailor questions meant this was a bad idea– but no, we've established that I was being a fool. A stupid, lonely, rejected fool.

Anywhere but here. The depths of the sea, an old creaky boat, it didn't matter.

An old man with a long gray beard and skin that looked like sun-worn leather squinted down at me. "What'd ya want?"

Oh, oh, this was it. Time for my line.

I'm here to respond to the ad for a seaman.

I'm here to respond to the ad for a seaman.

"I'm here for some semen!" I croaked.

Red embarrassment shocked against my cheeks as I stumbled

over my words, correcting myself, willing my tone into low self-assurance.

"Come aboard, lad," the old man called, passing me a rope as my feet left land.

"Yes, rope, I'm great with rope. And sails," I added as men eyed me briefly before carrying on with their duties.

I followed the long-bearded sailor, trying not to trip over the heavy ropes, as he chewed on a pipe. "Whatcha know about porridge?"

"Uh," his question was not on my list of study topics for pretending to be a sailor, but surprisingly I did in fact know a lot about porridge, having been on breakfast duty most every morning at the inn. "Lots, actually."

"You like rum?"

"Never had it, it uh, smells weird to me."

The man stroked his beard and regarded me as if I were a lunatic. I knew I looked and sounded like one. He was about as tall as me, and I was only five foot three, but he was all tendon and age, whereas I was soft and inflexible. The motion of the vessel as it rocked in the still of the dock was already causing me to wobble, and I assumed he noticed it too as he looked at my feet. "Trade boots with me and get into the galley. We set sail at noon. Men'll want their supper at sundown."

The weight of the rope pulled at my shoulders as I chased the weathered sailor down a narrow, smelly set of stairs into the lower part of the ship. He gestured to a small wood stove, sacks of potatoes and oats and other dried goods in sacks. "This here's the galley. I'm Captn' Fig, welcome aboard." He roughly took the rope from my sweaty, feeble grip and slung it over his shoulder.

His parting words slapped red across my face again.

"Holler when yer ready for that semen. Sure, there's several boys 'round here that would oblige. Though you dress strange for a lady, I don't think they'll care once we're good and out to sea."

My feet slipped on a wet slosh of saltwater, and I tumbled into a lumpy bag of potatoes as the ship jolted forward. There was no turning back now.

I'd never go back.

Never see her again.

Little did I know just how much I was leaving behind.

Chapter Two

THE GIRL

For the next several days, I barely emerged from the galley. That's another word for kitchen, and I'd learned several other words that sailors used. They talked in code. Some were not so savory. Clearly, my disguise was as weak as my current headspace because the few men that deigned to even notice me paled and didn't speak a word. At first, I was worried about the captain's semen joke having literal consequences. I wasn't interested in a tryst with a sailor, not when Rummy's hazel eyes were still so fresh in my mind. But then, as the few men who did get near me acted as if I had the plague, I began to get offended. Did I smell? If I did, it couldn't be worse than some of their joyous, sweaty aromas.

One evening as I sat on a crate peeling potatoes with a rusty pocketknife, prepping food for the next day, another task I'd adopted from my life working in hospitality, the usual clatter and stomps from above stilled. Something else graced my ears, and I ascended the staircase for the first time to the tunes of the men singing under the stars.

My throat dried at the vastness before me. And it sounds stupid. Again, we've established that I was very not smart at this point in time, but it was only then I realized I was out to sea. On a boat, leaving my home for some distant land, never to return.

The somber realization must have been written on my face because Captain Fig remarked, "You look hard up in a clinch and no knife to cut the seizing."

"What does that mean–" I began when a man interrupted.

"Don't make it talk!"

Another chimed in. "You've gone and fucked us all now, Fig. If this weren't a hell's mission anyhow."

The rough-looking man in a torn shirt shot me a look of disdain as he continued. "Sailin' us through the sugar seas on a fool's quest to the land of bells." He threw his apple core off the side of the ship.

Captain Fig shrugged. "Night's as clear as day. Maybe that sugar sea legend was all to keep us from gettin' the gettin' goods."

Again, they were speaking in some code I could only partially decipher. But it was clear my presence wasn't wanted aboard. The tone of the evening, and the steely look in the crew's eyes, sent a shiver of unease down my bones. But not only that, I hadn't even bothered to ask where we were going. I'd assumed this was a shipping vessel, delivering or fetching goods, and we'd sail to another island town. But from the conversation, a sense of dread settled over me as only the stars illuminated the partially visible faces of the dozens of sailors before me.

"Sugar seas? Land of bells?" I asked hoarsely when the captain flicked me a glance before taking a long swig of something that smelled awful.

"Crock of shit stories, girl. Pay them no mind."

The other man stood, his face hard and horrible. He pushed a rough finger into the captain's chest. "I've lost men to these very sugar seas we sailin' through this very minute. Friends of mine, family. None survived. Nothin' now but whispers of flesh-eating creatures of the deep, pirates that'll flay you out and use you as bait to catch one of the sugar monsters, songs of the tide that'll drive you mad…" He gave the drunken captain a shove and the old man toppled over easily onto the deck, not putting up a fight, but rather conceding to the moment. "You tricked us, lied, all for a chance to get to this fabled blood-stained utopia. Hell, we ain't even know if it exists. But," he pointed at me and my body froze as the ship rocked. "Somethin' goes wrong, I'm putin' the blame on you. Everyone knows it's bad luck to bring a woman aboard."

"She ain't aboard, Quintin," the captain argued, pulling himself up and wobbling forward. "She's below deck feedin' y'all sorry lot."

Quintin scoffed, passing me a hateful glance before grabbing a bottle of alcohol and walking away.

The men fell into conversation, some scattering back to their night duties, as trepidation followed me back down the stairs to my wet corner kitchen.

It was funny; I thought as sleep evaded me and I went back to shakily peeling potatoes, that I'd set out on such haphazard adventure, to find myself in almost the same place as I'd left. Alone in a kitchen, surrounded by misfortune and people that hated me.

Though the ones I'd left had reason to hate me.

This crew of sailors didn't, well, not any reason I'd given them other than just being a woman and I guessed that was just inherently unlucky whether on land or at sea.

As I drifted to sleep, my mind rippled with thoughts of what mystery lied beneath the creaking ship boards. What terrors could such an innocent name hold? The sugar sea. Had men really gone missing through this stretch of water that looked like any other, or was the sea captain right and it was just sailor ghost stories? Regardless, the land of bells awaited, and I had to make it there. A place to begin again, far, far away from her.

Chapter Three

THE GIRL

Oatmeal sloshed from my ladle into fourteen bowls the next morning, however, two bowls remained on the counter, clinking together as the ship rocked. I wondered if I were even allowed to go above deck, or if my womanly presence would curse the ship further. Stupid. Men were so stupid. Maybe Quintin was standing at the top of the stairs waiting for me to dare show my face again after his loud disapproval of my very existence the night before. Regardless, there were two men without food, and my little innkeeper heart couldn't stand the thought of one of the idiots going hungry. Maybe they were afraid to be near me. Afraid that some of my woman-aboard-a-ship bad luck would get them gobbled up by some man-eating fish. The idea made me giggle as I clutched the bowls and stepped into the jarring sunlight. The usual bustle of activity was lessened, and I looked around, not sure what to even search for. Boat life was all foreign to me. The top deck was always littered with ropes and metal things and water and whatever else.

"Who didn't get their breakfast?" I asked to the back of the men's heads as they looked over the side of the ship. They turned to me after a few moments, one taking off his hat and closing his eyes in prayer. Looking amongst them, I noticed some missing.

Quintin strode forward, and before I could react, slammed his fist against my forearm, knocking the bowls and shattering them to the ship's floor. "You tell us, *woman*. Who lost their lives last night because of you?" His voice was graveled and stern, and the look of murderous rage tightened my throat.

"Wh-what?"

Captain Fig intervened, "Men go overboard, son. It ain't the first time."

"It's the gods damned sugar seas!" Quintin shouted. "How many more men should we lose before we can't man the ship? All for her?"

"Go back to the galley," Captain Fig instructed me lowly, stepping between me and the giant, hot-headed sailor. He didn't have to tell me twice. I scurried away, frightened, and feeling guilty somehow. "We need her," I heard the captain say in a hushed and soothing tone behind me. And a new sort of fear settled over me.

The fear that not only was I ignorant to sailor ways and customs, but perhaps my presence aboard was too easy, too odd. There was so much I should have questioned, so much I should have thought through. I was an ignorant girl running away from home. And that ignorance was about to bite me in the ass in a big way.

The next morning, four additional bowls of oatmeal were unclaimed. Leaving the crew at only eight men.

Captain Fig swallowed hard as he clutched the captain's wheel.

"We ain't got much further if the stars are right." I heard him say when I creeped up to eavesdrop on the stairs. I wasn't allowed on deck anymore. And could only guess at what was transpiring each night that left men missing at sea. Was there a murderer aboard the ship? What other explanation could there be? Quintin had not appeared, but to my small and selfish dismay, I'd heard his voice berating the captain. Quintin was still alive, and I didn't doubt for a moment that if he saw an opportunity to end my life, he wouldn't hesitate.

Surely some sort of shore had to be nearby. We'd been traveling for nearly two weeks by my count. This land of bells should be near, surely, wherever it was and whatever it held remained a mystery. No one spoke to me, and the captain didn't come to check on me either. As the sun sank and the light below deck dimmed, I decided I wouldn't hide that night.

Men were disappearing somehow, maybe through murder, maybe through delirium, causing them to jump overboard. But I wouldn't be able to figure it out and possibly keep more of them alive unless I pieced the clues together for myself.

There were many times at the inn when the men wouldn't show up in time, with the wood for the fires, or with their deliveries of food or beer, and Rummy and I would have to make do and concoct a plan without them. We always did, always found a way to keep the stoves on and the inn heated. And I didn't come all this way to be stranded in the middle of nowhere. I didn't want to die... though my heart hurt as if it had been stabbed to death. I just wanted away from everything, the inn... if she could move on and have a brand new life, then so could I.

So, I sat. I sat at the top of the stairs, leaning against the wall as the ship rocked back and forth like a baby's cradle, the smell of rum and tobacco burning my nose as the wind flapped through the fabric of the sails. Waiting, waiting. For what, I wasn't sure, but I stayed in the shadow of the door and out of sight as the crew milled about.

"You hear her?" A man's voice asked softly, and my eyes flickered open.

Another man answered as I rubbed my temple. "Oh, she sounds so beautiful."

"Cover your ears!" someone shouted. "Grab the girl, I'm done with this– they can have her!"

There was a splash, and a man screamed, guttural and wet with something I suspected was more than seawater. My heart beat in my chest as I strained forward against the boat as it rocked roughly.

Droplets pricked against my face, and a bolt of lightning splintered across the sky. Mountains of water rose around us, striking fear into my being of the likes I'd never experienced before. The black tides furled around us, throwing the ship like a rag doll, and as I looked around the empty dock, I made eyes with the captain as he clutched the wheel of the ship.

"You've done it, you've damned us all! May the sugar seas take ye as an offering!" He yelled out, clearly drunk, with a crazed look in his eye. I stepped forward as thunder clapped so loudly my ears hurt. My foot caught on a rope, and I slipped, falling backwards. My head knocked against something metal, and then, everything beyond the thunder stopped, the rain lost its feeling, and all fear and panic faded away on the tide.

And then everything went pitch black.

Chapter Four

THE GIRL

I dipped my toes into the moonlit white sand. Rummy pulled at my palm. "The ocean is so gross and dirty. There are creepy things in there, too. Stay on land with me?"

"For a price," I smiled sweetly.

Rolling her eyes, she let me ease her forward and we kissed. Under the moon's glow, by the beach foam, and the skittering crabs, we kissed for the last time.

I wish I'd known it would be the last time.

A tap, tap, tap, vibrated the wood beneath my cheek. My bones creaked in pain as I wretched myself up off the wooden deck, meeting the beady eyes at a flapping fish. Why was a fish flapping on deck? Unless it had washed onto the ship from the storm, or something... I rubbed my forehead, squinting in the bright light and trying to stand but toppling over. We'd survived the storm, thank the gods. Pulling myself up by the side of the boat, I looked out over the ocean, half expecting to see... something.... Anything different. Anything except the blank and same expanse of water. No wonder the crew went crazy, it was as if nothing ever changed out here. There were no mile markers, no guideposts. For all your mind and body knew, you'd sat in the same patch of ocean every single day without moving an inch.

Oh, my gods, the crew.

"Hello?" I called out over the sloshing waters as the boat rocked. The captain's wheel was vacant of Fig and his grey beard. There were no crew atop the poles, and the ropes fluttered in the wind with no one to tie them. The sails flapped idly with every errant breeze. In a panic, I stumbled down the stairs and back up, finding nothing but emptiness. Slumping down under the mighty captain's wheel, I held my knees.

The crew was gone.

And I was alone on an unmanned ship.

Chapter Five

THE SIREN

Dipping my sharp claws into the water's holy surface, I smiled to myself as the little orange fish wove between the space left between the webbing of my hands. My sisters chattered, brushing their hair with fish spines. Their color was bright that day, after their sailor feasts, they glowed even in the bright sunlight above the sea. The sparkles of Edina's red scales, the glimmer of Cupida's pinks like a coral reef, and the deep aqua of Brizo's wet hair as it trailed next to her thick fin. We were the most beautiful things in the ocean. Not as matter of boasting or pride, a matter of evolution, it was simply a fact.

Us sirens used our beauty and temptation to lure our meals to us. Our prey were decidedly stupid, simple, ugly creatures on two legs, covered in prickly putrid hair in odd places. No fins to speak of, nevertheless, season after season, they ventured into our waters. Our bait laid and effective even without our songs.

"You are looking bright this day," Edina remarked, picking her fangs with a finger bone from the previous night's meal.

I surveyed my fin as it drooped off our rock and lazily into the lagoon. It shimmered amethyst that day. Though, unlike my sisters, my colors always changed.

I nodded. "I got the big one's heart. Oh, it was bitter," I chuckled.

"Lucky," Cupida cupped her bare breasts, admiring the way her light yellow-pink hair fell over their fullness. "His liver was decidedly tough. I only consumed half and fed the other to the hammerheads."

Brizo hissed. "A waste when I left hungry."

"You're always hungry," I quipped, eliciting melodic laughter from my sisters. "Remember the time you devoured a ship of forty on your own?"

Brizo smiled, her fangs still tinted crimson with blood. "The goddess of storms delivered such a mighty bounty that eve, didn't she?"

I loved sharing in sacred sirenhood with my sugar sea sisters. Edina and her curious and astute nature, Cupida and her innocence leading to great findings and many a meal, and Brizo with her ruthless and insatiable hunger. We were the wicked ones of the sugar waters. No other sirens inhabited this particular tide. Why would they bother? It was true that fewer boats came through here, perhaps due to our reputation, but still many did.

Edina stared wistfully in the distance, her orange gaze the color of first sunrise, her gills along her neck folding in and out softly. "I believe they seek out the blood lovers."

"Who does?" Cupida asked, rubbing Edina's hair gently.

"Our prey, the mortal men. I believe all of their kind seek out that which they cannot obtain, even to their ultimate demise. Though, we do them a mercy with their ocean deaths. Better their organs an offering to sacred sirens, than their blood an arousal to the cold tormenters."

Brizo dipped her tail in the ocean's tide and flung it at my sisters, splashing them. "You're as superstitious as the humans. Believing their archaic tales now?"

Edina shrugged. "Some night, sister, we'll catch a blood lover and you'll roll over on your gills."

My dark siren companion rolled her diamond eyes in response, opening her mouth to respond, when we were interrupted. Salmon hued tentacles sprang like seaweed from the waters around our sleepy rock. We extended our palms, quieting to listen as the suction of the octopus's gripped to the skin on our forearms. The tentacled being kept her head buried in the tide, opting to twist around us instead... the sensation... not unpleasant...

I want...

A low voice radiated into my mind. Though I couldn't be sure what she was communicating to my sisters. Cupida groaned softly as a tentacle twisted around her torso. My own breath hitched in my throat as his grip tightened around my neck.

Brizo answered whatever she'd communicated to her, "Not possible." Though her tone was edged, her tail twisted around the thick tentacle that pinned her to the rock, slithering up her middle. She bucked against it, her cheeks turning red.

Edina made no sound beyond the wet sound of slurping, as the tentacle thrusted into her mouth and she sucked, hallowing her pale cheeks. This was becoming a long-standing habit. Though we never knew when she would appear, and she never showed her octopus head, or form, and well... I supposed we didn't quite know what she looked like, for she always disappeared before we went back under the break. But her voice was smooth, her commands easy, and she left us sated in a way that tearing through human meat did not. No, those killings only calmed our stomach's hunger, not the deeper and insatiable desire we had to mate. And oh, as glorious as it was, there was little I desired to mate with in the ocean. Though, many things desired to mate with me.

Such was the siren's allure.

Sometimes I minded.

This time I did not.

Cupida called out, sounding like a flute played over still waters. Her voice, her everything, was the most beautiful of us. A tentacle pierced her entrance, which she readily unfolded her scales for. Brizo and Edina writhed beneath the touch of their unfurling and pulsing pleasure. It looked as if we were being controlled from below, the tentacles were our strings. Pulling our pleasure this way and that.

A deep, unearthly voice echoed in my mind.

Open your scales to me, siren.

I gasped as I was wrapped around the wet and bumpy mass, three, four times round, pinning my arms at my sides. "I don't like being told what to do," I challenged weakly, the tip of the tentacle rearing back and staring me down like a water snake.

Your body does. The creature retorted in my mind as it slowly sank to coax at my opening. The lips of my entrance throbbed with need and my scales, now fading from amethyst to ruby, parted like a gate, making way for what was to come. Immediately, the tip pierced me like a stake to a fish. I cried out, my own siren song weaker than my sisters. But together, our melody of pleasure haunted amongst the mists of the waves that lapped against our rock. The octopus being expertly drove my fellow sirens to release after release as it pushed in and out of me. And then, deep as it could go, it curved, pressing a suction cup over my bud of sensations. Pressing down hard before pulling up. Wiggling back and forth, sucking my bud as its tip pressed and spun within me. Somehow, I'd laid back, though I didn't even feel the cold hard rock beneath me. My back arched and I moaned, it sounding more like a song, our combined pleasure a wicked tune to no end. There were no sailors to hear our call, no human monsters to coax forward into the sugar depths.

I supposed this was just for us... and for her, whatever our newest friend got from the exchange, I couldn't know. Though she got what she wanted when we finished with the men. However, it seemed never enough. And thus, these exchanges began.

Once I'd came four times, the being slinked away, slipping back into the depths.

Fix it. Was her parting words.

I looked to my sisters, all in various stages of sated, blood flushed, lip parted disarray. "The ship still stands."

"That cannot be," Cupida replied, trying to tame her now unruly, curly, sunlight colored hair.

Brizo sucked in a breath. "'Tis what I said. Though, there must be one lowly coward left aboard."

Edina stretched her arms as she laid on our perch, still basking in the warmth of her release. "Not it."

"Not it." Brizo and Cupid said at once.

It was a game we'd observed and learnt from a long-eaten crew of sailors. They each declared it at a task they did not want, and the last standing had to attend to it. Annoyance pulled my ribs as I looked to the horizon. "Fine–"

But it was too late. The sirens had dove back into the sea. I'd sooner catch a stray undertow than one of them. We were fast; we were stealthy, and always hidden beneath these sweet waves.

Best of all, we were deadly. And irritation aside, I found myself panged with hunger once more. What's one more sailor to lure toward my teeth and claws?

We were death.

And this last sailor was mine.

Chapter Six

THE GIRL

I was going to die. I was going to eat all the porridge, and then I was going to die. Either a rogue wave would take me out, the ship would capsize, or whatever made the men flee would soon do the same to me. Hiding in the galley wasn't helping, but I found myself shaking, holding my knees, and crying. Thoughts of the inn danced through my mind. Chopping melons, tearing at coconut flesh, the drunken stories of the sailors that came by. Now, I sifted through those stories like a hand of cards.

Some warned that the worst you'd find would be the ocean monsters, ones with long triangular teeth and pointed fins. Some more massive still, with long ropy arms that could grab you and steal you away. I shuddered at the thought of one of those lurking beneath the very wood I sat. Worse yet, others warned... were the pirates. Gods, no. I'd never met one, and yet their stories were spoken about in more hushed tones than the monsters. And I was sure they were real. I wasn't as positive about the monsters, but pirates were not a figment of sun poisoned boat work. What if pirates had taken the crew?

That didn't even make sense. Not when I replayed the events of the storm. The men were acting strange before that, though... none of it made sense. But regardless of what the answer to the riddle was– I was alone on a ship I didn't know how to sail, in the middle of the ocean.

Furthermore, I was a coward, hiding in a kitchen.

No, I was back at the inn, back at the stoves, fixated on the patch of flour on Rummy's tan cheek... I swallowed, realizing I'd never see her again. Wasn't that the point of coming out here?

No, the point was a new life, not to find my death. Though the men with me had found theirs... unless maybe they'd gotten on another boat and stranded me for some reason? My head was fuzzy as I slowly ascended the stairs into the waning sunlight. It was close to suppertime; it would be dark soon. Would the monster or pirates come back for me?

The sound of something beating against the wood startled me. A rope swung free, hitting a post, while a sail sagged, limp in the ocean breeze. I'd only caught glimpses of the crew going about their chores, and I'd immediately regretted not paying closer attention to what they were doing. But I was fairly certain the rope shouldn't be spinning around and hitting things. I grabbed it and pulled it tight, wrapping it in a weak knot around something metal and heavy on the dock.

Wiping my brow, I walked up onto the platform and stood at the captain's wheel. The ocean looked beautiful from up there, I realized, and I wanted to get higher. Finding the ladder, I climbed the same sail post I'd seen the men do, and held tightly onto the top, looking out over the miles and miles of water. Hope sprang and vanished in an instant when no land was to be seen. There was no way to know what direction I was headed, and the waves rocked the boat. One more storm, one more bad decision from me, and I'd be going down with the ship.

I stayed there for the longest time, watching the sun dip and cast the most radiant shade of orange and purple along the shadowy depths. When my eye caught something, it shouldn't have.

Something not real.

It was... a woman. A woman treading water mere yards from the ship.

My heart leapt into my throat, and I called out, "Hello?"

A song, a wordless, beautiful song, flitted through my ears. Like an angel, like an instrument I'd never heard... high and feminine and so haunting it broke my heart. My hands were shaking as I climbed down, seeking it, seeking her. I had to help her. Who was she?

The melody continued, and I climbed.

Forgetting the stories.

Forgetting the sailors' warnings.

Forgetting what the men had heard the night before.

I climbed down toward my death.

Chapter Seven

THE SIREN

I'd sang, and sang, and no men emerged. The depths were calling me home when there was motion at the ship's captain's wheel. What little coward had stayed behind? Who was stupid enough to evade my song, my tumultuous allure? My throat squeezed, and I'd felt I'd been caught in a net when I first saw her.

Her?

She didn't smell like a male, no, decidedly female scent. Not male, decidedly female.

It had never crossed my mind that these humans had females. I know that sounds like nonsense. But I'd never considered it. They never brought them on boats, I'd assumed they were land animals, not made for water. Though men weren't either. My logic was weak. Edina would know more, would have the answers to human breeding practices. All I knew was she was... the most beautiful thing I'd ever seen.

Across all oceans of coral, all jewels and pearls, every shimmering fish scale and blue clear waters with schools of color. Against every sunset and sunrise unwitnessed by any eye but mine... she was the most stunning of them all.

And she did not hear my song.

I swam closer, not bothering to conceal myself, needing to see more of her. That hair the color the waves leave behind on the sand of the shore... it brushed against her bare, sun reddened shoulders that were covered in similar colored spots. Goddess, I needed to see the shade of her eyes, her lips. What was happening to me? No sailor had ever so much as tempted me back. But this... this female human...

Before I knew what was happening, a new song hummed from my throat. One I'd never before sung, but it was lovely, and ghostly. Perhaps being a siren leant itself to different ballads for different beings? Things I should have known but never had the occasion to care about. I wasn't like my sister Edina, whose thirst for knowledge kept her exploring, seeking, and learning. But now, as I watched the woman climb and her eyes finally met mine... all I wanted was to know her. I wanted to know everything about her.

The water warmed around me as she finally heard my song. Did she like it? Surprise shocked her features as she called out, waving her arm at me as she approached the side of the boat.

I understood her words. The goddess who blessed sirens with song also gave us the talent of understanding all tongues. It came in handy when following boats, listening to the male humans loudly shouting their routes, their plans, how many aboard. But the tone of this woman's greeting was light and airy as a salty breeze and not the crunchy rocks of men's voices. Oh, I wondered what her song would sound like if she sang? The thought had my center and hips tingling above my long fin. Could I coax her into singing for me?

She leaned over the side of the ship and said again. "Hello? How-how are you out here?"

Did she not see me for what I was? I looked down at my arms in the fading sunlight. My color had changed again, now mirroring her own pearl skin tone. Noting I could use this to my advantage to get closer to her, I pulled my hair, which remained black as the deepest sea, over my shoulders to hide my gills. Yes, I did look like a human woman from the waist up, like a harmless mermaid. Just a lonely human woman washed out to sea... *yes, come closer, come talk to me sailor girl...*

"Hello," I repeated, for lack of a more eloquent greeting as I swam closer, careful to keep my fin hidden. "Are you alone?" I asked.

The girl gave a perplexed expression before deciding something silently before replying. Her gaze caught on my breasts, and she swallowed. "There are no men aboard. You'll be safe with me," she answered, extending her hand, though it didn't reach me. A gesture of trust, of safety, that's what she offered a strange ocean woman. She offered me safety from men. *Safety from men.* Did their females fear them? All the better that I ate their innards if one ever struck fear into this lovely being or any like her.

What an odd creature this female was aboard a dead ship. The reason the octopus creature wouldn't, or couldn't, claim it, I presumed. The reason I was sent to kill her. And I could have right then. Her spotted arm extended, hair wavy with salt air, already lured close by a siren song made just for her... I could take her and see what female organs taste of. See what *woman* does for our bodies and spirits, it could be something divine and rare, giving us more strength and power than before.

But I felt a pull to her that I couldn't explain. Like a hook in my cheek, reeling me forward like a guppy on a hook. A lust and attraction I only ever received and never reciprocated. Was this how men felt for me before I drowned them? What an intense and fascinating sensation. Though I did want to taste her. Oh, so badly I wanted to taste her perfect, shell-pink little mouth. Was a human woman's sex in the same place as ours? How odd and horrifying it must feel to not have a tail. No fins, no claws, no fangs. This poor thing was here all alone...

"You poor thing," she said softly, repeating the words I just thought to myself. "How did you get out here all alone? Is another ship nearby?"

"What is your name?" I asked back, still making out the color of her eyes. Soft, lily pad green. Exquisite.

She shook her head slightly, still confused. "Please, let me pull you onto the boat."

"Why do you cover your breasts?" I asked, noticing the fabric draped down her form, hiding her body.

Her face flushed a crustacean shade of red. Could her skin change color like mine? Or just her cheeks?

"Excuse me, why are you exposing yours?"

"They're beautiful," I replied plainly. "Should any of the sea hide her artistry?"

She showed her teeth with a smile. They were flat and not pointed like mine. It made sense that humans had to catch fish with hooks; they had no other way. So defenseless, these creatures. Worry slithered into my chest. How would she survive? I'd taken down many boats with my sisters. I'd listened to years' worth of men's work as they toiled upon the ship's deck. It took many of them to control one of these contraptions and their massive, cloud-like tops.

The sun sank over the horizon, washing everything dark without the sun goddess's light. "I'll light a lantern. Stay here, okay?" The girl instructed before slowly backing away as if she were afraid of taking her eyes off me. At that moment, a thick fin brushed my tail, and I knew the hammerheads had arrived. They expected scraps of sailor bodies, but this night I would have nothing to feed them. Sparing my sailor girl one last look as she disappeared, I fell beneath the water's surface, petting the heads of the sharks as I did.

"Next time," I promised them.

I came to lure, to kill, to give the tentacled creature its due... I swam into deeper waters with no organs, no boat to give, and only an ache in my heart that I didn't want to leave her. She had to survive. There had to be a way to help her. Oh, how was I going to keep her alive in these sugared seas? The most treacherous of tides, storms, and worse yet, of beasts such as me. I had killed so many of her kind, I had no idea how to keep one alive. But I would find a way. I had to find a way.

Chapter Eight

THE SIREN

I returned the following day, tossing a myriad of bounty onto the ship's deck. The girl screamed, but then ran to the ship's side, cheeks flushing again in that way. I just wished I could get a closer look.

"You're back," she let out a breath. "I thought you were a dream... or that you'd drowned."

Humans had dreams? How endearing. She was so adorable I could hardly tolerate it. A soft chuckle purred over the waves as I laughed. "No, I could never drown." My gaze whisked over the clouds and concern eased into my being. I'd never charted the weather in the way a sailor might, but I knew when the storm goddess was getting restless, and I couldn't fathom my girl surviving one of the goddess' more magnificent onslaughts.

"Why are you throwing fish and crabs at me?" she shrieked, looking at the deck in bewilderment.

I stayed back a suitable distance, but the water was clear, the sun bright, and if she looked closely, she would see... Though I would love to see her too… "I'm feeding you." I replied plainly, swimming closer. "Won't you come a little closer?"

Her lily pad green stare shot to mine. I recognized that look, the look of fear. I was the last thing so many of her kind saw. Surely the warning resonated in her blood. Or perhaps my siren charms were doing their job and tempting her closer, because she obeyed, leaning over the ship's side. Through her terror, she scanned the water, her eyes then ascending to my breasts again. "You're a–"

A rogue wave slapped the ship with a splash. Her hand slipped, her knee slipped too, and ripples of information caressed me as she splashed headfirst into the sugared seas. I sank, waiting for the bubbles to clear, and regarded her and her horrified expression as she took me in. Her cheeks were round with air, like a pufferfish, that soon left in a flurry of bubbles as she screamed under the tide. Her arms thrashed about, her legs moved with no reason, and sea wood hued hair fanned around her as I swam closer, running my long-clawed fingers through it as she squinted, perhaps expecting their sting rather than the gentleness I rarely offered.

This poor, beautiful mortal.

When she paled, I realized humans couldn't breathe underwater. Of course. I was forgetting myself.

I pulled her to my chest and dragged her above the surface and into the salty air. She gasped, coughing, and clutching her arms around my shoulders. The feeling of her soft body pressed to mine was… not unpleasant.

"Mermaid!" she choked out, trembling against me as the waves rocked us high and dipped us low.

I smiled, and apparently that was the wrong thing to do, because upon seeing my fangs, she screamed again.

"No, no," I assured her, willing my voice into a soothing tone. She calmed for a moment. "I am much worse than a mermaid."

Another scream. I wasn't good at comforting humans, apparently. How could I be when I was created to do the exact opposite? My very existence was sending tremors of shock through the human girl's body.

"Are you going to eat me?" her voice cracking as she shook in my hold.

I tilted my head, mesmerized by the tiny spots on her face, her tender warmth, her little hands holding onto me. "I'm going to keep you." I replied definitively.

She swallowed. "Keep me?"

"Yes."

Her tiny, clawless fingers slowly slid over the gills on the side of my neck, and my eyes fluttered closed in pleasure. "Oh," she gasped. "You're purple now. You change color?"

I nodded.

"You're beautiful," she murmured. "Did you... are you the reason the crew is gone?"

My jaw tensed, and I realized she was cold. Swimming to the side of the vessel, I noticed a tiny boat tied to the side of the ship. The tide was high, and the boat wobbled in the water as it clanked loosely against the larger ship. I lifted her with ease; the water rising around me in aid, and sat her gently in it. The feeling... was wrong. She should be with me always. But how?

I swam backward, and she reached out. Her ripped blouse clinging translucent to her breasts. Mmm... there they were... my own cheeks warmed at the sight.

"Wait, please don't go," she begged softly. "It's okay if you did... they weren't the nicest of men."

I raised a skeptical eyebrow. "A human woman who does not fancy her own males? I can relate to that sentiment."

"I never have." She rested her chin on her palm. "You're red now," she said idly. "And I'm going to die out here."

"You won't," I corrected adamantly. "I'm going to help you."

"How?"

I looked around, feeling the breeze, smelling the air and scouring my brain for information. What little I knew would aid her until I gathered more intel. Pointing toward the horizon, she followed my claw. "Human land is that way, but very far. Tie the bindings in the opposite direction, so the wind pulls you that way... but untie them at nightfall. It's going to rain."

Her eyes widened. "Is it... going to rain hard?"

"Not this time. But it will soon."

The sound of the waves nodded their agreement. We did not have much time to get her to safety.

"I will be back to check on you soon." Before I could dip under, her touch on my chin startled me.

"Thank you," she whispered. "You're pink now."

I leaned into her touch... I'd never been regarded in such a way. This human girl was... magnificent. Careful to show a nicer smile, I bid her farewell, and swam in a direction I did not want to go.

But I needed guidance... the kind that came with a price.

Chapter Nine

THE GIRL

I'd already blown out all the lantern flames and was retreating to the warmth of my bed when one rainy night a knock pounded against the inn's door. When I opened it, a man stumbled inside, grabbing onto my nightgown. My white gown smeared with blood as he coughed and clutched his chest. My instinct was to run away or shove him off from shock. But he was pouring blood and begging in incoherent sentences. "The story keepers," he coughed. "They be coming."

"What?" I asked, falling to my knees under the weight of him before crying out for Rummy or an inn guest to come help. As he died, laying on the floor as a storm raged outside, he cupped my face.

"An angel," he said, his eyes glazing over. It was the last thing he uttered before he died of sword wounds. I thought of him often. Of how he came to be so injured, of why he fell and died at our inn, and what he must have saw as his body gave out. He thought he saw an angel, or that maybe I was an angel, come to guide him to death.

It occurred to me as I pulled the ropes tight, watching wind fill them and pull me toward the horizon, that maybe my mermaid monster was my angel. Maybe I'd hallucinated her in my dying moments aboard my watery casket. She was a figment of my imagination, come to guide me to death. And truly, she was breathtaking. The most stunning woman–er–half woman– I'd ever seen.

My ocean angel.

When she left, I'd thrown the fish back overboard. I never had the heart to kill them. The crabs I left, letting them roam and clatter along the deck. They were better than being alone. Doing what my ocean angel instructed, the boat began a slow sail in the direction of... I had no idea. This went on for three days. I'd hear fish flapping against the wood, and my heart would beat in tune, eager to look over the ship's edge and see her. What color would she be? What strange and horrifying thing would she say? Why did I have an overwhelming desire to jump into the water with her? She'd outright admitted, or at least not denied, to killing the crew of men–yet somehow my fear of her waned the moment she gazed at me with those terrifying and beautiful eyes.

She looked like a human from the waist up, perfect breasts that competed with her eyes for my attention. Slits on the side of her neck that rippled like the waves with her color changing skin. The only shade that remained fixed was her long, inky black hair. My ocean angel was stunning, and I couldn't look at her long enough, even in the hours we would talk as the waves rocked and she fretted about how to keep me alive. I was sure now I would likely not stay alive, though, if she were the one guiding me to death, death wouldn't be so bad.

The ocean was my watery grave, and my siren's arms were my casket.

It was then I realized I hadn't thought of Rummy in a week. Not since the appearance of this sea siren. And though I was sailing on a ship doomed for destruction, for the first time since my feet left the sand, I was happy. How tragic and wonderful all the same.

Chapter Ten

THE SIREN

The orange fish wiggled in my mouth as I clutched it enough to hold but not puncture with my fangs. I wanted to save the blood from my little human to drink. Though crabs were in short supply as I sifted my webbed hands along the sandy ocean bottom.

"Where have you been?" Brizo's voice echoed behind me. Panic seized my shoulders in the knowledge that I'd avoided my sisters for far too long, keeping this ship and its sole occupant a secret.

I grunted an unintelligible response when Cupida fluttered by me, twirling between two sapphire jellyfish while giggling. "What are you doing to that unfortunate fish?"

Edina swam backwards with a book in her hand, the flick of her fin scattering across the sand and halting my crab search. I stopped with annoyance and crossed my arms. "I'm busy," I muttered curtly.

Brizo narrowed her gaze, her fin looking a deep shade of green that suited her well. "There's a new boat coming by tonight. I trust you've taken care of the last one?"

I swallowed, feeling her barracuda stare. "It's taken care of." Not entirely untrue... I *was* taking care of the ship and its one inhabitant.

"How'd he taste?" Brizo pressed, giving the yellow fish between my teeth a flick with her claws.

Cupida and Edina eyed me curiously, both distracted enough from their activities to monitor our conversation. Rolling my eyes, I kicked my tail, jolting toward the surface. "I'll see you tonight at the new boat." My retreat was swift, as I was very fast. We all had our gifts, my sister sirens and me. Perhaps I wasn't as beautiful as Cupida, as smart as Edina, or as fierce as Brizo, but my speed was greater than that of a swordfish. And goddess, I was thankful for that blessing then.

Thoughts of the incoming boat schooled through my mind. Another kill, another feeding, would typically send me swimming with happiness. But now it filled me with dread. We'd kill, and convene with the tentacled one, and then what? What would it say?

And then another startling thought trailed the fish-school of questions. Why did we care? Why were we answering to this being?

I passed a pod of friendly orca whales before reaching my sailor girl's ship. The whales were kind and whistled their warning of an incoming storm. I nodded, blessing them with my touch. A storm was indeed coming, a great one, and the sea rumbled and rose softly in quiet anticipation. It would be thrashing above the surface in several days, and I knew my new friend could not survive it on her own. Her ship was not moving quick enough, was too far from land, and the boat itself wasn't equipped to take on an onslaught of waves. This was a conundrum that had to be solved quickly and with more than thrown fish and crabs.

Her gorgeous face appeared the moment I'd flung the fish, and her boat stilled, bobbing in the water. "Wait!" She called, and I leveled my eyes with the sea's surface. I had more to do, more options to explore in keeping her safe. But her voice calling out to me... was this what men felt when I sang their slaughters to them over the night waves?

One leg hitched over the side, then the other, and she unbuttoned her blouse. I arched an eyebrow, but before I could question, she jumped. A smile bloomed across my features as I went under, watching her move her arms and legs, and slowly approach me on her own.

When she reached me, I grabbed her, pulling her warm body close, our noses touching. "You're swimming," I whispered.

"I've been practicing so that I can swim with you," she replied.

I pulled back slightly. "You shouldn't practice without me. The sugar seas are very dangerous."

"Dangerous because of you?" Goddess, her spots. I wanted to count them all.

"Because of me and other creatures. Some you know, some you do not."

"Can you tell me about them?" She asked.

My gaze flicked to the boat. I should leave her and seek more aid, somewhere, somehow... but she felt so nice in my arms.

"Hold on," I instructed, positioning her on my back. "I swim very fast," I warned.

She giggled lightly. "I love going fast."

With a laugh of my own, I sped just below the surface, feeling her breasts against my back and my hair tangling in her body as we reached our destination. A rock, in the middle of the tides. There were few of them, and they were only visible at certain times of day, whenever the moon and sun goddesses allowed them to breach the waves. To our luck, it protruded into a flat surface, and my sailor girl climbed atop it. "Sit with me?" She asked, smiling, and I obliged, pulling onto the sun-warmed stone next to her. I ran my claws through her long brown hair, and she did the same with mine.

"Within the tides of the sugar seas are sharks the size of your boat, with teeth as big as your hand. Though they stick to the depths, they wouldn't hesitate to take a bite of you."

She swallowed, and I continued. "There are fish that sting, impale, and strangle. Then there are the hidden ones, the ones like me. Siren and mer folk, tentacle monsters with insatiable appetites. Beyond those, beneath our city, there are the dark ones. Beings who've stolen magic from the goddesses, and it has corrupted their minds."

Her eyes widened.

"So, to answer your question, yes, there are things in this ocean scarier than me. Well, at least creatures less enticed into submission by beautiful women as me, I suppose. You will not swim alone again; I am commanding it."

My girl nodded, and the sound of her heart speeding up flitted through my ears. When the salt air breeze blew, I believed I smelt her arousal, and it was a storm that only amplified my own. "Goddess, I want you," I breathed, inching toward her lips.

She stilled, strands of my black hair falling through her soft little dull and clawless fingers. "Can we?" she asked on a hopeful breath.

"We can and we will," I answered, pulling her body to mine. My palms found her breasts, my thumbs rolling her hard nipples. We both sighed into our passionate kiss. I flicked my long tongue into her mouth and she groaned, pushing her hips against my fin. My fin snaked between her legs, all the way to wrapping around her ankle and holding her in place until she was on her knees with me between her. "That's it, use my fin, my beautiful sailor girl."

I eased my grip down her sides, carefully minding my claws so as not to mar her delicate, thin skin. She felt like the softest sand on the warmest day under the sea foam. Her taste was like the sweetest dew from the rarest ocean flowers. She held my arms for balance as she thrusted into my fin, and I rippled it in response, moving my scales up and down to hit her sensitive spots just right.

Her soft moan of release rivaled the most pure of my siren songs as her bliss found her. The melody was mine now, for all the days of the sun and sea. My sweet sailor girl mating with her siren, our scents meshing together as one, forever entwined by this moment.

I wasn't near fed, needing more of her, desiring to taste her. "Take off your clothes," I ordered. My red-cheeked, spotted sailor girl obeyed, standing on the rock and kicking off her pants, and unbuttoning the rest of that silly white top. How I longed for her to always bare her breasts as freely and proudly as the goddess she was. Slipping my tail and torso off the rock and into the water, I laid back and beckoned her forward. "Kneel over me and let me taste you."

She hesitated a moment, eyeing my sharp fangs, and I smiled. "Ah, yes, my teeth are pointed, but not nearly as horrid as my tongue." I unfurled my long, forked tongue and let it drape down my neck in wordless promise of the pleasure it could provide her.

A small gasp escaped her lips before she slowly straddled my face. Taking my hands for balance, she bent her knees, and my tongue did not hesitate. I pierced her entrance, and we both groaned. My sailor girl was wet with need for me. The sweet nectar of her arousal danced over my tastebuds, finer than any ocean flower I'd ever tasted.

"You feel so good," she panted, rocking over the base, as the forked tip pulsed and devoured her from the inside.

I moved my hands up the sides of her hips when a sound from the water pulled another gasp from her throat. My powerful, long tail propelled from the water and snaked above me, over my head. The tip of my long fin finding her bud of sensation.

Her moan, another melody I'd earned, was beautiful over the rippling ocean. The tip of my fin stroked her, swirling wet salt water over her center, while my tongue worked and spun inside her opening. This time when she came, her own bit of ocean followed after her. Her release poured over my face, and I drank in its sugared waters greedily. She was more delicious this way than if I'd decided to feast upon her organs. Surely, this way, I could feast upon her over and over again.

"You are... the most delicious human I have ever tasted." I awed when she collapsed into my arms.

Twilight glittered in the calm sugar sea as I slowly brought my girl back to her ship. I let go, laughing as she held tight to my neck and I peeled her grip away. "Try to swim on your own, little strange and beautiful creature."

She flailed, kicking and smacking her arms against the surface of the water, straining to keep her chin afloat. How sad and pitiful to only be able to breathe above the waves, a whole beautiful world she would never see, my entire pearlescent city she'd never enter. My heart cracked in my chest.

"I hate this," she complained, spitting, and bobbing as I circled, learning her movements. This gorgeous spotted human was mine now and I would learn how to care for her. Even if we came from two different worlds, even if her skin was dainty while mine was hard. Her dull teeth could never saw through fin or bone. The nubby fingers on her hands were without fins or claws. My poor, sweet creature. How would I save her?

"Perhaps with practice you will swim better," I encouraged. "Some of your kind were able to dive to the ocean floor for oysters and crab. Many men were fair enough swimmers before I killed them."

She shrieked before giggling and reaching for me. I took her in my arms then, wrapping my fin around her protectively.

"Why didn't you kill me?"

"Because you're mine."

Her cheeks reddened. "You're purple again. You're purple a lot with me."

"I never notice my own shades. My sisters are much prettier than I am."

"You have sisters?" She asked inquisitively. "Can I meet them?"

My jaw tightened as if I'd crunched a fish bone. What would become of this ill-fated union between a sailor girl and a siren that cared for her? My ocean community, my sea family, wouldn't understand such a love. I suspected Edina would be cautious with her vast knowledge of humankind. Cupida would be curious... but Brizo... I shuddered at the thought of Brizo ever learning of my newfound mate.

Cradling my sailor girl in my arms, I kissed her neck, inhaling her scent and marveling at the melody of her sigh, stopping outside her boat. Thunder rumbled overhead, and she held me tighter as the waves answered the sky's call. "Please—"

"What is this?" A sharp voice interrupted behind us. I swirled around, pulling my girl onto my back and pressing her against the hull of the ship. My hair couldn't hide her. It was too late, as Brizo and my sisters swam closer.

Brizo clicked her long serpentine tongue against her pointed teeth. "You've lied to us. You're harboring the remaining man."

Edina and Cupida gasped, cornering us.

"Climb onto the boat," I whispered, feeling my girl tremble upon my shoulders.

"I don't want to leave you." She gripped me closer, burying her little face into the crook of my neck.

"You must," I urged, holding my palms to my sisters. "Not a man, never a man. This is a female."

Brizo's glare was harsh and deadly and it raised both fear and fury in my soul that she'd dare stare at my mate in such a way reserved only for our prey. "One of *their* females," she bit out. "The reason the ship could not be claimed."

"Why do we care if a ship is claimed by a monster? Have you asked yourself that, sisters? In my days away from the lagoon, these thoughts have become clearer. Since when do sirens aid unknown creatures? We do not need them, but what do they need of us?" My family only gazed over my shoulder as my girl finally obeyed, climbing over the side of her ship.

At the last moment, Brizo lunged, and my girl screamed. I intercepted my sister, grabbing her hand and hissing in her face. "Don't you dare. She is my mate."

The sirens gasped.

I continued. "I'm keeping her. She is mine, and you will not sing to her, nor touch her. Say you understand me?" I pleaded in the furious and terrifying face of Brizo, who looked as if she wanted to rip out my eyes.

Brizo glanced up at my girl before snarling. "They take our fish and they tarnish our ocean. There is a reason the goddesses bestowed the honor of the siren upon us—and this is how you repay their gift? By saving one, by *mating* with one?"

"A *woman*." I held her shoulders, begging her to hear my words. "Never a man, not one of them."

Brizo's glare softened only slightly as lightning cracked the sky and a scream tore amongst the darkening waves.

Two screams.

Brizo gasped, pushing us apart as a spear shot between us. My girl shrieked, and a knife pressed to her neck. I hissed as a man held her tight, surveying us.

"No!" Brizo shouted, pointing. Pulling my gaze from my girl, my heart and fins frozen in panic. Cupida hung by a net, several men reeling her in as she tossed and fought.

"Those are the men you fight for!?" Brizo growled in anger as Edina held onto my arm in fear.

My voice shuddered as I beheld my girl in horror as she tugged against her captor, and my sister twirled and tangled in her net, hissing and clawing as men leered at her.

"Not men," I breathed in sorrow. "Pirates."

THE GIRL

The cold of the knife mixed with the slick wind. My stance wasn't as steady as the man that held me captive and my attention flicked from him, to my siren, to her blond sister trapped in a net. Chaos, this was chaos and... I noted the skull on the black flag of the ship that pulled next to us. Fear stabbed me in the gut.

Pirates.

My weight was no match for the pirate that gripped me, my siren and two others were snarling as they circled the boat and disappeared and reappeared above the waves.

"Mermaids!" the one that held me shouted.

Another scruffier pirate came up behind him and hit him on the back of the head. "Not mermaids... Sirens."

"Gods help us," my pirate captor breathed in my ear.

That was my opportunity. Balling my fist, I used all my might to hit my assailant in the groin. He swore, dropping the knife and tumbling over. I quickly grabbed the knife from a puddle on deck and positioned myself between the siren that hung from the net and the pirates. The ship rocked as a few moved like a dance, manning the sails, tossing ropes. Their movements fluid and practiced, nothing like that of the men I'd first sailed with.

My captor, the scruffy man, and someone else—someone wearing a black pirate hat, sauntered over. Then my eyes met his--- no —*hers*.

"Well, I'll be damned. A sailor girl and a siren. It's our lucky day, boys." She tipped her hat, disregarding my shaking knife. "I'm Captain Calico, and you've just been captured by the Pirate Keepers of Stories."

The siren behind me shirked back into the net and I caught a glimpse of a pirate throwing a spear into the water. "Stop!" I called out, ignoring the captain. "Don't hurt them!"

The woman raised an eyebrow, and through a bright flash of lightning, I made out her long, curly red hair. "They're the ones who wish to hurt us, lass."

Just then a melody twisted through the electric air, dancing over the waves, somehow a softer yet more audible octave than the sea and storm themselves. The pirate captain swore and covered her ears before shouting at the man beside her. "Crank the juke!"

I glanced over my shoulder as my back bumped into the large, pale pink fin of the siren behind me as she dangled like a beautiful canary in a cage. She eyed me with curious suspicion as I still held the knife in the direction of the pirates. "I'll protect you," my teeth chattered together in cold and fear.

Before I could receive a response, a man screamed, and another jumped off the boat, as the captain scrambled to the side of my ship, shouting demands at the larger pirate ship next to us. "The juke!"

The few men on our boat were jumping overboard, only their screams signaling their watery deaths. Suddenly we were enveloped by an unnatural, neon green light, and the floorboards vibrated with... music? It was coming from the pirate ship. Captain Calico turned on her boot, wiping her brow and pulling a flask from her vest. Horror washed over me as the thumping sounds of rock music drowned out the sirens' call, and the pirates cheered from the other ship, slinging ropes, and tying our boat to theirs. Like a lassoed animal, we were tethered together.

The siren behind me hissed as the captain took a step closer, assessing her, ignoring me as I jabbed my knife forward in warning. Captain Calico drawled after taking a heavy swig of rum. "Magic jukebox. It drowns out the call of all sorts of ocean beasts such as this one. I reckon we'll fetch a high price for this beauty, won't we?"

"Don't get near her," I threatened. "What is it you want? Money? Gold? I can find a way to get you that. Where I'm from, my inn, it has money—"

The pirate ran a confident, seductive finger down the top of my slick blade as a snarl rattled behind me. "Did you not hear me, girl? Not just any pirates came to your aid this day. 'Tis not gold or riches we seek."

Chills pricked the back of my neck as a lithe and melodic voice spoke, for the first time, over my shoulder. "Stories," the siren answered. "You want stories."

The captain's face lit up, and she gave a small, sideways smirk. "That's right, beautiful. And you will give me everything I want. Won't you?"

Chapter Twelve

THE SIREN

Brizo's screech was sharp and thunderous as she thrashed like a shark in a blood frenzy. Edina circled the ship, ripping the throat from a pirate before shredding through his skin in search of his organs. I didn't want to feed, couldn't think of it, not with my girl and sister trapped aboard their vessel with the rest of the monstrous men.

As we broke the surface, an abnormal sound rumbled atop the sea and we were washed in blinding light. "What is that?" I called to my sisters, as our siren song proved ineffective. Edina, cocked her head as we waded, the men cheering and leering at us as if they'd just won some sort of game against our ocean goddesses.

Edina's eyes widened. "I've read of these... but I fear if my research is correct, that these are no ordinary pirates. These pirates... they are that of legend amongst both land and sea. Goddess help us."

Brizo smacked the top of the water in anger before pointing a claw at me. "This is all your fault. Our sister ensnared by these creatures while you laid the bait!"

"I'm sorry—"

"I will fix this. I am always the one to fix my sisters' mistakes." Brizo jeered.

I swam closer, ignoring the hooting and hollering of the men. "What does that mean?"

But with only an answering glare that would freeze a charging barracuda, my fierce sister sank below the tide. Edina took my arm and pulled me under, safe from the gawking of the pirates. I spared a final glace at Cupida as she swayed in her trap, like an ordinary fish. My girl standing in front of her, fighting to protect my own kind. My heart swelled and splintered in pain. Brizo was right, I'd disappointed my sisters, and I'd failed my mate.

"Where are you going?" I asked as Edina dove deeper.

She twirled. "Research."

Of course. In a crisis, we all reverted to our most instinctual states of being. Brizo to her rage, Edina to her knowledge, and me... what did I offer? Swimming. Even a guppy could do that. With a discouraged sigh, I trailed beneath the ship, watching the neon lights change from green to pink, and praying to the goddesses that I wouldn't see a splash of bubbles at any moment—indicating my sister or my girl being tossed lifeless overboard. In my time of meeting my sailor mate, I'd lamented at how powerless she was. Yet now, I found myself to be the feeble one. My claws, fangs, and fins—even my song—were no match for pirates. What use was I? Just a fish following beneath a mighty whale and waiting.

For the first time in my life—I longed for legs. I would have traded my scales in a heartbeat if it meant saving her. And in that moment, when the water glowed purple from the pirate's magic ship —I realized I was deeply drowning in love.

Chapter Thirteen

THE GIRL

'd fallen into a fitful sleep. Lulled by the rock of the boat, the warmth of the siren at my back, and the commotion of the pirates and the storm. No one locked me away, no one paid much attention to me at all. So I slumped into fatigue, and my mind played tricks on me as I dreamt. As I dreamed, I remembered.

"You're getting married?" My mind spun. There was no other woman Rummy had kissed or been with but me. I didn't understand.

"At sunset, on the dock."

"I don't understand... I thought we were—"

Rummy took my hands. "We are great friends."

Pain stabbed my heart. "Friends? Who—who is she?"

With a furrowed brow, my friend dropped my hold. "He is a lord... I will be running a household, I won't have to work at the inn, I can have children--- please, you must see how this is best—how you should find the same—"

"A man? You—we—how could you? We were to run the inn

together for all of our days. You said you loved me. We have made love,
Rummy."

"I'm sorry... you are only a friend to me."

Only a friend. A friend.

She'd married him that evening, as I watched on sobbing. Afterward, I stumbled back to the inn where they were to have their feast and their first wedded night. I grabbed the discarded men's linens, changed from my dress into sailor pants and a button-down shit. Then, I'd struck a match, and lit it all on fire.

I'd watched it burn. The rooms we'd made love *as friends* in. The kitchen we'd kissed *as friends* in. The stairwell she told me she loved me *as friends* in. It was all gone. And so was my life.

I wanted to die beneath the waves rather than watch her become a lady of a house and marry and have babies with a common man.

Now, I'd get my wish for a watery death. Now, I felt I never loved Rummy at all, or at least, I'd never known true love with her. The kind that's felt back, the kind of love that isn't one-sided desire but mutual adoration and care. It was what I felt with my siren of the sea. The very ocean I wished to drown in now sent me its angel to consume me with love—but the most wicked thing of all was I'd never be able to be with her.

How could a girl of air and a siren of sea be together? We were more doomed than Rummy and I ever were—or maybe less— knowing that there was a chance my siren loved me, too. Would I ever find out? Did she leave me for dead? No matter, I'd use my last days to make sure her sister swam free. Captain Calico was sharper and more perceptive than what I'd imagined a pirate to be. Maybe these were a different breed of pirates—not in search of gold—but in pursuit of tales of the sort even sirens knew of their conquests.

My natural inclination was to run away and hide... but now... things were different. This time, I would find another way. For my siren, I would find another way. Could I best the surly sea captain? I'd sure as hell try.

"Ye want me to move them aboard, Captain?" The hairy pirate asked. We were the only ones remaining on the captured ship, and the others, men and women, I noticed, were manning the dark grey pirate ship. It was more worn and weathered than this vessel, though larger and more sinister looking.

Captain Calico eyed me and the siren thoughtfully before responding. "Somethin' tells me they should stay here—and me with 'em. You go man the main. Shouldn't be but a few days before we're out of these cursed sugar seas."

A few days before we left the sugar seas? Panic and sorrow clawed at my heart. I couldn't leave my siren. What if I never saw her again?

Chills rose the hair on the back of my neck and arms as I recalled the pirates spearing the waves. What if my siren was hurt? I slumped onto the slippery deck next to the pristine siren within her net. The rain pattered to a misty drip around us as I idly watched the surly sea captain tie ropes and adjust sails.

"You should go with them," the beautiful siren said softly next to me. Her voice like melodic wind chimes on a cool summer breeze. "They're your kind. They can get you to land."

"Pirates are not my kind."

"Humans are."

"Well, I don't claim them anymore. And I'm not leaving you. I'll find a way to set you free if it kills me."

The siren tilted her head, and I allowed myself a faint moment of getting lost in her rose and turquoise eyes. "I'm Cupida, that is my name. And do not dismiss your mortality so quickly. I have spent many sopping, swimming days wondering what a life on legs might be like." She smiled, her rose colored hues twinkling before adding. "My sister loves you. I feel it in my gills."

My cheeks flushed. "I love your sister and that means I love you, too, by default. I'm not leaving you to a bunch of asshole pirates."

The siren shrugged. "Something will come for us, perhaps the mer, perhaps the sea... perhaps something far worse. But Captain Calico will die with a lungful of saltwater from my seas."

She seemed so calm, so unworried, that her assured words shivered me to my bones. And apparently, I wasn't the only one, as Captain Calico dropped something heavy, noting us when we looked over, before quickly tucking her wild red hair behind her ears and securing another rope.

Clearing her throat, she walked over, taking a sip from her flask and offering it to me, which I denied. The Captain then eyed the siren and offered the drink, which to both of our shock, she accepted. We watched in fascination and horror as the siren opened her mouth wide, unhinging her jaw like a serpent and baring her sharp fangs before swallowing the flask whole.

She licked her lips with a pink, forked tongue. "Disgusting."

Captain Calico doubled over with laughter, putting two hands on her knees as she howled. I bit my lip to hide my smile as she dried her tears and knelt before the siren. "I like you. What's your name?"

"I don't have one."

"You won't be freed by lying. I know lies, I know truths, I am a story keeper." Calico replied evenly. "And I'm finding myself inclined to keep you alive."

"The feeling is not mutual."

Again, the captain laughed, lowering to sit cross-legged. I inched backward, content to pretend to be asleep while the two talked. I had to find a way, hatch a plan, to get us both back to where we belonged... and... where did I belong again? That was the question, wasn't it? I'd figure it out with a lungful of air or... like the siren sister said, a lungful of saltwater.

Buzzing rock music and men laughing from the other ship galloped over the waves. The siren chimed, "I'll use your bones to pick my teeth. You think I've never tasted story keeper pirate before?"

Captain Calico arched a half smile. "It would be an honor to have you taste any part of me."

"It would seem as if your little music box of nonsense doesn't work against my song, then, Captain." She reached a long, slender arm through the netting, beckoning the pirate closer. Despite her claws, the captain crawled forward, and it was an effort to pretend my eyes were closed and my middle wasn't heating at the sight.

Would Cupida take the opportunity to cut the captain's throat? Her long claws cupped the pirate's jaw, bringing her closer. "A taste, you say?"

The pirate's eyes hooded and her lips parted in desire as the pink siren cupped her face, claws tangling in Calico's red curls. I half expected blood and half expected sex. A tantalizing combination.

Even though the ship shook abruptly and I wobbled right onto my butt, I couldn't take my eyes off the two of them. For a moment, it was like staring at me and my siren from the outside in. Is that what we looked like? Though I doubted my own beauty even came close to the surly captain or the serene siren, they were lovely to look at on their own, yet together... they were a stunning sight to behold. They reminded me of a sunset over the ocean. Captain Calico, the bright and burning sun and the pink siren, the fuchsia waves beneath the ruby light.

It was wrong, because the red-headed woman currently in a lip-lock with the beautiful blond siren was our captor, but I liked the two of them together.

Suddenly, the pirate captain drew a knife, holding it above the siren's head. I screamed in warning, trying to get steady on my feet before lunging forward. But it was too late. Captain Calico sliced, and the siren fell to the ship deck, the net splayed around her as she still clutched to Captain Calico's neck. The pirate had cut the net, not her lover, and still held her by her pink finned hips.

"You've bewitched me— and I've let ye." Captain Calico purred into another kiss.

Cupida flicked her long tongue playfully against Calico's neck before shimmying out of the webbed netting that blanketed them. "Now, it's only fair you allow me to drown you and feast upon your flesh."

The siren made it sound as if her words were a seductive promise and not a threatening and horrific fate. Somehow she spoke to the same fate I looked over the bannister and into the depths at. There were no other options for me. I could die in the sea with my siren or I could live a half life on land.

Captain Calico only seemed excited by the idea of death as she pressed her body closer to her siren and they began to move together. I felt I shouldn't watch, so instead I looked over the ship's edge, content to jump if I saw my own purple, raven-haired beauty.

An unfamiliar pair of eyes met mine. Glowing turquoise in the deep, as if she were lit from within, she spoke to me. "It would be better if you gave yourself to me. I could make a necklace of your bones to give to her, my sister, whom you desire... but Cupida needs to be freed. If any harm comes to her, I will kill you most painfully, sailor girl."

I swallowed. Another sister of my siren, though this one seemed... fiercer, angrier. The boat rocked again and instead of lulling forward, it slammed to an abrupt halt. Captain Calico appeared next to me then, Cupida at her side, pulling up onto the edge of the ship's banister by her elbows. Her mighty tail swished calmly. Despite her sweet exterior, I had a feeling that this pink siren was just as crafty as the clever sea captain.

"Another siren? It's as if you're all obsessed with me." Captain Calico tossed her red curls over her shoulder. "To what do I owe the pleasure?"

"Give us our sister back now, or later, you die either way." The blue siren snarled from where she waded in the dark waters. Men from the other ship shouted, touting their spears, but the captain raised a hand to silently stop them.

She ran a tender hand through Cupida's long blonde and pink hair. "What if I like her? I do enjoy collecting beautiful things... and the stories she could tell..."

"Brizo," Cupida said in a sing-song voice. "I'm having a bit of fun. Don't be so worried. A female pirate. How delightful. I've never seen one before."

Brizo crossed her muscular arms. "Playing with your food is about to get us in a load of trouble."

Just then, my siren appeared, and my heart leapt. Each time I beheld her, she was more stunning than the last. I wanted her. I knew in that moment, no matter what. If only it meant a lungful of water ushering me toward my death.

Swimming closer, glowing from black to her glittering shade of purple. Opening her mouth to speak, I gasped at what happened next. Even the pirate captain shouted and Cupida shrieked.

An enormous tentacle shot from the tide— wrapping my siren in its coils before dragging her beneath the surface.

Chapter Fourteen

THE SIREN

Though I'd been the teeth of the predator so often, bringing death to men and fish alike, I'd never considered my own end. I was at the top of the food chain in the ocean, in the world, what could stand against a siren of the sugar sea?

As the creature squeezed my middle, my gills constricted and my ribs threatened to break— I had a myriad of thoughts swim by like a school of fish.

Fish number one: the tentacle creature that had been toying with my sisters and me for goddess knew how long was in fact— the thing wrapped around me like a sailor's rope.

Fish number two: as it pulled me deeper into the depths I caught sight at the sheer size of it. The largest of any being I'd ever seen in these waters.

Fish number three: it was a kraken, and it was going to kill me.

Fish number four: as it shot me back out from the ocean, I saw the pirates running about frantically. That was humorous, at least.

Brizo held her head in anguish and rage. This was her doing, wasn't it? Maybe that's fish number five.

I'd resigned to death until I saw my sailor girl. Taking a dagger from the red sea captain, she bit it between her teeth and climbed the edge of the ship— and dove off. Swimming near me.

"No!" I shouted, though my breath was thinning. My gorgeous, perfect, sailor girl was on a death swim. If the kraken didn't kill her, Brizo might, or one of the sharks that followed after us. She needed me, and I could not die, would not die unless it was to save her. I sent a quick prayer to the goddesses. I hadn't prayed in a long while, knowing our siren prayers were numbered. Was this the last prayer I was allowed?

Allow a trade, begin a new life.

It was not the most thoughtful nor poetic prayer like the goddess deserved and required— but it would have to do.

The kraken pushed me above the tide, only to slam me back into its mighty waters again. Through the bubbles and chaos and screams, I saw her. My brave sailor girl swimming toward me. Pride swelled in my chest at how she'd heeded my instruction and was swimming stronger than ever. When she reached us, she didn't hesitate. Despite having no gills, she grabbed onto the kraken's suction tube and plunged the blade into its coil. Black, inky blood sprayed and to my surprise, it uncoiled, releasing me.

I grabbed her immediately into my protective hold and shot to the surface to provide her with air. My fragile sailor girl— now so fierce, so courageous.

A wet gasp sucked into her mouth as we broke the surface, and she panted, holding me tight. I rubbed her hair, softly kissing her head as I looked on in horror at the scene before us. Trying to shield my sailor girl to no avail, she turned and clutched me tighter. "It's—it's taking down the ship?" She asked in terror as I moved us a good distance away.

"It is angry with us for denying its feed. The pirates will die as well."

Just then Brizo shot from the water, so camouflaged I had no idea how long she'd been there or been listening. "Help," she hissed. "Cupida is in there!"

"Why is Cupida in there?" I shrieked, instinctually moving my girl to hold on to my back. "You brought it here, didn't you? You sought the great kraken."

Brizo narrowed her gaze at my girl and a hiss the likes of an eel propelled from my fangs.

Brizo answered, "I did what I had to do to remedy the mess you made." She pointed a long, harsh claw. "You brought humans to us and not in death. It is not the way of the ocean."

She was right. It wasn't. I was going against the waves, the goddesses, my lineage of sacred siren.

"She is my *mate*," I whispered as the ship cracked and men screamed. "I would forfeit the sea for her."

My sister's eyes widened, finally taking me seriously. "Then I will stay with her. You are the fastest swimmer. You retrieve Cupida."

I didn't like that plan. Being away from my sailor girl did not feel right. But Brizo was right, I was the fastest swimmer, and whatever kept Cupida in the thrashes of a kraken devouring a ship must have been something that required my swift attention. Reluctantly, I moved my mate's wrists from my neck and passed her to my sister.

"I'm trusting you, Brizo," I said in silent plea and warning.

With a curt nod, she cradled my girl, and I looked to my mate with uncertainty.

"Go, I'll be okay," she assured, though her expression told a different tale as she watched on as flame erupted from the cracking ship.

I'd made it with lightning speed that rivaled the barracudas I used to race as a child. Wood and rope sank around me as I dodged the heavy poundings of the eight massive tentacles. The kraken's mouth was open, showing twelve rows of teeth as big as I was. A shudder racked through me as I wove between debris. The kraken was taking the ship my girl had been on, as the other pirate ship fought to get away. Smart of them, and I only saw a few bodies of pirate sinking to their new purpose— shark food.

But where was Cupida?

Suddenly, I caught a flash of pink and yellow in my periphery. I'd been searching below waves, but for some reason my sister was above the tide. Narrowly dodging a heavy and jagged beam, I was at her side. She was holding something and crying. "Sister, I can't leave her."

"What— who—"

Cupida held the body of a woman above the wave, but the human's eyes were closed. "This is the Story Keeper Pirate Captain Calico— and I love her."

Shock and confusion muddled my mind. This must have been what Brizo felt when I announced my mate. "Cupida... she is a human. She has no gills, no fins, no claws—"

"I know that!" she hissed, frantic as the Kraken thrashed around us. Finally, Edina appeared, and I hoped she would help me to talk sense into our love-struck sister. Edina has always been the intelligent one amongst us.

"Where have you been?" Cupida accused sharply, still holding her red-haired human above the waves.

Edina looked between us, mildly offended at Cupida's tone. "Gathering knowledge that might benefit us, as always, sisters. I see it is quite a mess here."

Cupida sobbed. "I'm sorry, Edina. It's just— I want to be with my pirate. I want nothing more."

"There are ways..." Edina pondered before a tentacle crashed next to us, raising the tide and separating us. "We have to get out of here!" She shouted, swimming away.

We followed her, and I began to hope.

I began to hope until I heard my sailor girl scream.

Chapter Fifteen

THE GIRL

Brizo held me like I used to hold dead rats I found in the inn before ushering them into the garden for the crows. This sister siren was formidably strong and terrifying to behold. I almost felt pity for the countless sailors she had lured into her sharp grip. Surely their end was the most painful.

Brizo spoke over the rough waters. "We have magic, us sirens. Did you know that? It is materialized by our song, though the spirit of the ocean lives within us."

"That's amazing," I answered. "You're each very special."

She nodded. "You desire to stay with my sister as her mate, correct?"

"I do… is that even possible?"

Brizo glanced around, scanning for something, I wasn't sure. "There are stories of men becoming mer when they drowned in pursuit of a mermaid that loved them. If you're sure my sister loves you… there's only one thing left to do to test that theory."

"Die?"

A current slammed between us and Brizo let me go, swimming leisurely backward and blowing me a kiss goodbye. I made to scream, but it was a pale whimper as my mouth filled with water and an undertow sucked me into a cyclone of bubbles, pulling me deeper and deeper beneath the surface.

I'd come to terms with the fact that I would soon die a watery death— I'd just hoped my siren would have been with me when I did. I wished I could kiss her, feel her soft purple skin one last time. Had Brizo truly believed their legend, or had she only wanted me dead? It didn't matter, as the oxygen burned from my lungs and the sea from below grew darker and darker. My mind was blurry. I was fading— when a slash of red broke through the current and grabbed my arm.

She pulled me out of its grip and up toward the surface. The waves were wild then, and we were closer to the kraken. Every thrash it made as it still slowly savored its ship, rocked the ocean and seemed to make the waves angry.

The pirate captain held me, shouting over the violent waves. "We fell in love with sirens, lass. Together, we go down with our ships."

I didn't know what she meant until I looked up and saw a mountain. No, not a mountain of dirt, a mountain of sea— a wave larger than I'd ever knew possible, was looming and growing in height and force above us. It would take out the rest of the ship, it would stop the kraken— but it would bury us alive. There would be no surviving it.

In the distance, I thought I saw her— my amethyst sea goddess. She was swimming to me so fast, but she would be too late. I forced a small smile and squeezed Captain Calico's hand. "For the sirens of the sugar seas."

Her freckled face chuckled in return. "To Davy Jones' locker we go, lass. Perhaps a mer will take us to a door."

She spoke nonsense, but I was thankful to have the pirate to hold on to. My siren shrieked a mournful melody, and I thought I heard her sister Cupida do the same. As the mountain of a wave crashed into us. Swallowing us whole.

Calico held tight to my hand for as long as she could before it was pried away by the sheer and insurmountable force of the tide. I was pushed so far, so deep, my back hit something solid. Was it sand? Water overtook my lungs and in my delirious last moments of life, I opened my eyes and was in the arms of my raven-haired siren. With a kiss on my forehead, she tried to save me, but she was too late.

With my last breath, I pushed my final words through my throat. *I love you* became just another bubble in the great world of the ocean. A sentiment that would become the tide and be erased by it at the same time. Love was a massive, all-encompassing thing— it was also walking a plank to your end.

Somewhere in the distance, as I faded away, my siren sang an eerie and forlorn song. Cupida joined her. And something about it tugged on my soul. Sirens could lure sailor men with the songs to death... could they lure the woman they loved from death toward life?

The song continued, and my body felt strange as she held me. Somehow larger than before, somehow floating easier, my limbs not fighting between sinking and floating. Though my eyes were closed, I feared to open them and find that I was no longer here, no longer inside my body. Maybe my soul was floating above the tragic scene and watching as we left this earth.

My face felt sunshine, and the ocean settled. My siren ran her hands through my hair. I raised a hand to meet hers and my fingers felt strange. Opening my eyes, I first noticed my hands were now webbed. My siren smiled and wrapped her long tail around mine and pulled it above the water. "You're remarkable," she awed. "And you're mine forever."

My tail? My tail was light green and shimmering. The upper half of my body remained the same, aside from my webbed hands. I touched my neck. There were no gills. I felt my teeth for fangs, nothing. My tail was not as long or thick as my siren and I looked at her with confusion. "What has happened?"

"The goddess, the ocean, has given you a gift." Her smile was the most beautiful thing I'd ever seen. She let go of me then, and I didn't sink. I had so much control over my body it was as if I were my own boat in the water. Finally, strong within it instead of at its unrelenting mercy. No, I was a part of the ocean now.

"I'm not a siren?" I awed, spinning my tail around and admiring the sparkling emerald scales.

My siren came close and unbuttoned my tattered shirt and dropped it into a wave, letting my breasts hang freely. A naked woman from the top up, a long green tail from the waist down. "You are not a siren, my love. You are a mermaid."

A laugh of glee fluttered from my throat. "We can be together now?" I asked, full of hope.

"Forever," my siren answered, pulling me in for a kiss. "There is a whole world I cannot wait to show you, my love, my brave sailor girl."

We kissed for a few moments before I pulled away, noticing the pirate captain and another woman on our sunning rock nearby. "Who is that with Captain Calico?" I asked, relieved the pirate captain was okay.

My siren grinned. "Come, I'll show you." Instead of cradling me, she let go, and fear gripped my chest— until I remembered what I was now. My fin moved, I moved, cutting through the water as if propelled by magic. I sucked in a breath under the waves, the water not invading my senses but a part of them now. I laughed. "This is amazing."

My siren smiled on at the rock, where she waited for me to take my time in exploring my new body, my new skills. A mermaid. I was a mermaid now.

I reached the boulder and rested my head in the lap of my siren's long purple fin. "Captain Calico, thank you for coming after me. You saved me."

"I collected a story once," the sea captain answered, not looking away from the nude woman beside her. "That the ocean goddess likes trades... I figured she owed me a favor."

"What do you mean?"

Cupida sat up, and finally I recognized her, but she looked different. She kicked her long, pale legs, and wiggled her toes. "I'm going to have to learn how to use these things now."

I gasped. "You're human now?"

With a giggle, she smiled. "Between the sirens and the captain's pleas, it looks like the ocean offered us a bargain. I am human, you are mer."

"Pirate," Captain Calico corrected. "You're my pirate queen, now." They kissed softly, knowing their love had changed everything.

My siren ran her fingers through my hair, knowing the same. Our love had transformed what was impossible for something magical. What should have been was— and we would indeed be together forever. I looked out at the ocean that now looked just as big, but not as scary as before. My new home, my new world.

My siren slipped into the water and held my hand. "Where would you like to go?"

"Anywhere with you."

"Then that's where we'll go, my little mermaid."

I'd come to the sea to escape a love that couldn't be. Only to find a more impossible love awaiting me. This would be a love I'd never run from again, couldn't run from now that I had fins. My beautiful siren held me close, wrapping her tail around mine as we kissed. She was my forever.

I'd found a love that didn't hide me in back rooms and leave me in confusion. I'd found a love that offered me the whole ocean proudly, that took my hand, that taught me to swim it.

And they made their home in the deep ocean and tied in the warm sea of knowing their love was a love of depths the waters could never reach. Love was love, and love would always hold the power to transform what was into what *could be.*

A human loved a siren, and the ocean gave her fins.

Afterword

Most all of my stories come to me in dreams, and this one was no different. So vividly I dreamt of a purple siren chasing along a ship and picking off the men one by one. When finally she reached the last on board and was stunned to see a woman for the first time. The most beautiful thing she'd ever seen, and now she wanted to save her, to keep her.

And so Sirens of the Sugar Seas took form as a sweet little nautical treat. It is so much fun to play in whimsy and I loved our sailor girl and siren together.

No, they never gave me their names and I really like that. Oh, I wanted their names, begged and pleaded, but they never gave them up. I respect their choice and think it adds to the ocean fairytale of it all. They didn't need names to love each other.

I've always been obsessed with ocean lore. Nods to sharks, pirates (any halloween boy readers catch the easter eggs?) and spending time in the ocean was such fun.

Thanks for playing mermaids with me.
Until next time.
XO,
Kat

LADY VENOM TAKES A MISTRESS

Sapphic snake monsters

THE HALLOWEEN BOYS SERIES

Bisexual spookiness

Ghost

Dragon

Wolf

Devil

SELAH GOTHIC

Dark priest romance

Follow my siren song

• Sign up for my newsletter to be the first to know about new book releases

　• Join my patreon for NSFW art, early chapters, secret projects, and more.

　• Join me on #spicybooktok TikTok: @katblackthorne

　• See fan edits on Instagram @katblackthorneauthor

　• Follow me on Amazon for upcoming books:

　• Join my reader coven on FB Kat Blackthorne and the Black Hearts Coven

　Business or press inquiries please email katblackthorneauthor@gmail.com